NOT NOW, BERNARD

NOT NOW, BERNARD
A RED FOX BOOK 978 0 099 24050 1

First published in Great Britain by Andersen Press Ltd,

Andersen Press edition published 1980
Sparrow edition published 1980
Beaver edition published 1987
Red Fox edition published 1990

43 45 47 49 50 48 46 44

Copyright © David McKee, 1980

Red Fox Books are published by Random House Children's Books,
61-63 Uxbridge Road, London W5 5SA,
A RANDOM HOUSE GROUP COMPANY
Addresses for companies within The Random House Group Limited
can be found at : www.randomhouse.co.uk/offices.htm

THE RANDOM HOUSE GROUP Limited Reg. No.954009
www.kidsatrandomhouse.co.uk

www.rbooks.co.uk

A CIP catalogue record for this book is available from the British Library.

Printed and bound in China

NOT NOW, BERNARD
David McKee

RED FOX

"Hello, Dad," said Bernard.

"Not now, Bernard," said his father.

"Hello, Mum," said Bernard.

"Not now, Bernard," said his mother.

"There's a monster in the garden and it's going to eat me," said Bernard.

"Not now, Bernard," said his mother.

Bernard went into the garden.

"Hello, monster," he said to the monster.

The monster ate Bernard up, every bit.

Then the monster went indoors.

"ROAR," went the monster behind Bernard's mother.

"Not now, Bernard," said Bernard's mother.

The monster bit Bernard's father.

"Not now, Bernard," said Bernard's father.

"Your dinner's ready," said Bernard's mother.

She put the dinner in front of the television.

The monster ate the dinner.

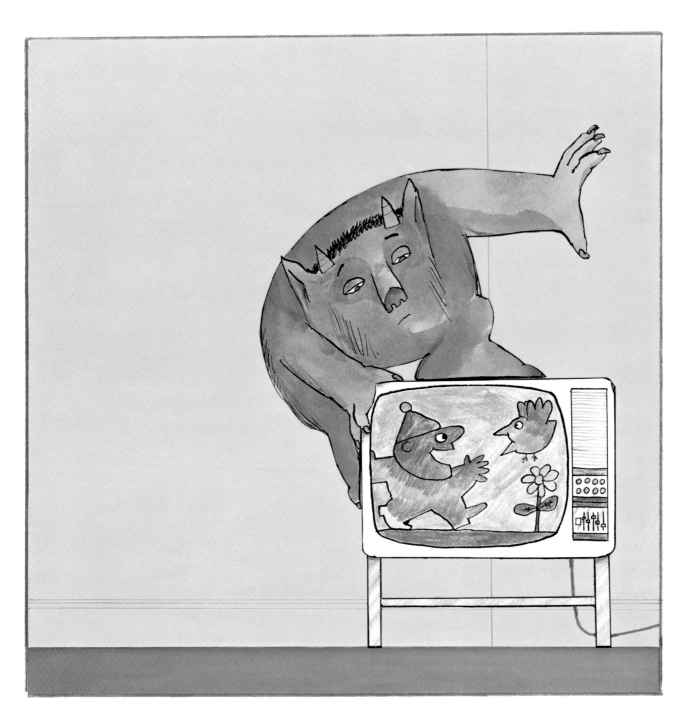

Then it watched the television.

Then it read one of Bernard's comics.

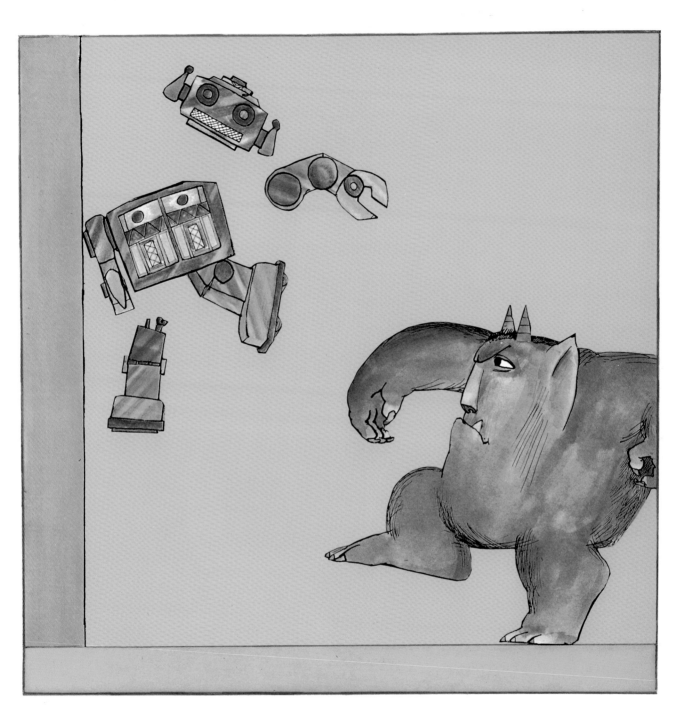

And broke one of his toys.

"Go to bed. I've taken up your milk," called Bernard's mother.

The monster went upstairs.

"But I'm a monster," said the monster.

"Not now, Bernard," said Bernard's mother.

More Red Fox picture books
for you to enjoy

MUMMY LAID AN EGG
by Babette Cole 978 0 099 29911 0

RUNAWAY TRAIN
by Benedict Blathwayt 978 0 099 38571 4

DOGGER
by Shirley Hughes 978 1 862 30805 3

WHERE THE WILD THINGS ARE
by Maurice Sendak 978 0 099 40839 0

MISTER MAGNOLIA
by Quentin Blake 978 1 862 30807 7

ALFIE GETS IN FIRST
by Shirley Hughes 978 1 862 30783 4

OI! GET OFF OUR TRAIN
by John Burningham 978 0 099 85340 4

Other books by David McKee